The traditional telling of fairy stories is part of every child's birthright. These tales of magic and adventure contain simple morals and satisfy the young child's demand for justice. Cruelty and evil are seen to be punished; fundamental to each story is that right triumphs over wrong.

Few popular collections of fairy tales are researched right back to the time when they were tales for telling in the true oral tradition. This selection of the most popular stories has been specially researched and written **for reading aloud to children.**

The author has successfully tried these stories with a large number of children of all ages. The full colour illustrations are in different styles to suit each story. But the magic is in the telling!

Contents:

2	The Story of the Three Bears	30	Three Billy Goats Gruff
7	Jack and the Beanstalk	34	Sleeping Beauty
16	Sly Fox and the Little Red Hen	38	Snow White and the Seven Dwarfs
20	The Three Little Pigs	46	Red Riding Hood
25	Cinderella	50	Rumpelstiltskin

Sources

The author and publishers wish to acknowledge the original sources which were used in the retelling of these stories:
Cinderella and *Sleeping Beauty* by Charles Perrault (1628-1703); *Snow White and the Seven Dwarfs, Red Riding Hood* and *Rumpelstiltskin* by the brothers Jakob Grimm (1785-1863) and Wilhelm Grimm (1786-1859); *The Three Little Pigs* and *Jack and the Beanstalk* by Joseph Jacobs (1854-1916); *The Story of the Three Bears, Three Billy Goats Gruff* and *Sly Fox and Red Hen* from the traditional tales.

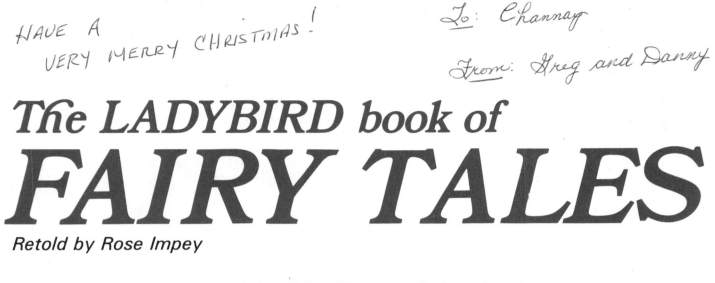

The *LADYBIRD* book of
FAIRY TALES

Retold by Rose Impey

*Illustrated by John Dyke, Brian Price Thomas, Robert Lumley,
Eric Winter, Harry Wingfield and Martin Aitchison*

Ladybird Books Loughborough

The story of the Three Bears

Once upon a time there were Three Bears, who lived in a house, in the middle of a wood. One was a Little, Small, Wee Bear; one was a Middle-sized Bear, and the other was a Great, Huge Bear. They each had a bowl for their porridge; a little bowl for the Little, Small, Wee Bear; a middle-sized bowl for the Middle-sized Bear, and a huge bowl for the Great, Huge Bear. They each had a chair to sit in; a little chair for the Little, Small, Wee Bear; a middle-sized chair for the Middle-sized Bear, and a huge chair for the Great, Huge Bear. And each had a bed to sleep in; a little bed for the Little, Small, Wee Bear; a middle-sized bed for the Middle-sized Bear, and a huge bed for the Great, Huge Bear.

One morning the Three Bears made some porridge for their breakfast, and poured it into their porridge bowls. Then they walked out into the wood until it cooled. While they were out, a little girl called Goldilocks came to their house.

Now Goldilocks was not a very good little girl, and when she came upon the house, in the middle of the wood, she was very curious. First she looked in at the window, then she peeped in at the keyhole, and when she saw that the house was empty, she lifted the latch and walked in.

Goldilocks looked around to see what she could find. On the table were three bowls of porridge. They looked very tasty, and Goldilocks was feeling hungry. First she tasted the porridge of the Great, Huge Bear, but that was too hot for her. Then she tasted the porridge of the Middle-sized Bear, but that was too cold for her. And then she tasted the porridge of the Little, Small, Wee Bear, and that was neither too hot nor too cold, but just right. It was so good that she ate it *all* up.

3

Next Goldilocks looked around to see what else she could find. By the fire there were three chairs. First Goldilocks sat down in the chair of the Great, Huge Bear, but that was too hard for her. Then she sat down in the chair of the Middle-sized Bear, but that was too soft for her.

But when she sat down in the chair of the Little, Small, Wee Bear, it was neither too hard nor too soft, but just right. She sat back in it so hard that the chair broke, and down she came, plump upon the ground, which made her very cross indeed!

Then Goldilocks, that inquisitive little girl, went upstairs to see what else she could find. In the bedroom were three beds. First she lay down upon the bed of the Great, Huge Bear, but that was too high for her.

Then she lay down upon the bed of the Middle-sized Bear, but that was too low for her. But when she lay down upon the bed of the Little, Small, Wee Bear, it was neither too high nor too low, but just right. She covered herself up, and lay there so comfortably that soon she fell fast asleep.

In less than no time the Three Bears came home. They were very hungry, and ready for their breakfast. There were the bowls still standing on the table. Now Goldilocks had left the spoons standing in the porridge of the Three Bears.

'Somebody has been eating my porridge!' said the Great, Huge Bear in his great, rough, gruff voice.

'Somebody has been eating my porridge!' said the Middle-sized Bear in her middle-sized voice.

'Somebody has been eating my porridge, and has eaten it all up!' cried the Little, Small, Wee Bear in his little, wee voice.

Next the Three Bears looked around to see if anything else was wrong. There were the three chairs. Now Goldilocks, that careless little girl, had forgotten to put the chairs straight when she sat in them.

'Somebody has been sitting in my chair!' said the Great, Huge Bear in his great, rough, gruff voice.

'Somebody has been sitting in my chair!' said the Middle-sized Bear in her middle-sized voice.

'Somebody has been sitting in my chair, and has broken it!' cried the Little, Small, Wee Bear in his little, wee voice.

Then the Three Bears thought that they had better look upstairs to see if anything else was wrong. There were the three beds. Now Goldilocks, with her meddling, had pulled the pillow of the Great, Huge Bear out of its place.

'*Somebody has been lying in my bed!*' said the Great, Huge Bear in his great, rough, gruff voice. And Goldilocks had moved the pillow of the Middle-sized Bear.

'*Somebody has been lying in my bed!*' said the Middle-sized Bear in her middle-sized voice. But when the Little, Small, Wee Bear came to look at his bed, there was the pillow in its place, but on the pillow was Goldilock's head, which was not in its place, for she had no right to be there.

'*Somebody has been lying in my bed – and she's still here!*' cried the Little, Small, Wee Bear in his little, wee voice.

It was such a sharp, piping, little voice that it woke Goldilocks up at once. When she saw the Three Bears standing there, she was very frightened. Quick as a flash she jumped out of bed, raced down the stairs and out of the house. Into the wood she ran, as fast as she could, before the Bears could catch her. What happened to Goldilocks no one can say. But of one thing you can be sure, the Three Bears never saw her again.

Jack and the Beanstalk

Once upon a time there was a poor widow, who had a son named Jack, and a cow named Milky-White. The lad was lazy and careless, and could never keep a job. All they had to live on was the milk the cow gave, and since the cow was getting old, there wasn't much of that. Then one morning Milky-White gave no milk at all, and they didn't know what to do for the best.

'Jack,' said his mother, 'we must sell Milky-White, or we will surely starve.'

'Sell Milky-White, mother? That seems a shame,' said Jack.

'Well, shame or not, the cow must be sold,' said his mother. 'Today is market day, so off you go. And mind you get a good price for her.'

'All right, mother,' said Jack. 'You leave it to me. I know what I am about.'

So Jack took the cow's halter in his hand, and off he went. He hadn't gone half way when he met a farmer, who said to him,

'Good morning, Jack.'

'Good morning to you,' said Jack, wondering how he knew his name.

'Now, Jack, and where are you off to?' asked the farmer.

'I'm going to market to sell the cow.'

'Well, you look a bright enough lad to know a bargain when you hear one,' said the farmer. 'I wonder if you know how many beans make five?'

'Two in each hand and one in your mouth,' said Jack, as sharp as a needle.

'Right,' said the man, 'and talking of beans, what do you think of these?' He pulled out of his pocket a number of strange-looking beans. 'Since you are so sharp, I don't mind doing a deal with you – your cow for these beans. What do you say to that?'

'Go along,' said Jack. 'I'm no fool.'

'I can see that,' said the man. 'But you don't know what kind of beans these are. These are magic beans. Plant them at night, and by the morning they grow right up to the sky!'

'Really?' said Jack. He looked at the beans, and he looked at the man. He was sorely tempted. Truth to tell, Jack had a real longing for adventure, and these beans seemed to be just the chance he needed.

The farmer could see how things stood, so he said, 'I'll tell you what; if it doesn't turn out to be true, well, you can have your cow back.'

'Done,' said Jack and he handed over Milky-White's halter, and pocketed the beans.

Then Jack headed back home, and since he hadn't come far, he hadn't far to go.

'That was quick,' said his mother. 'Now then, what did you get for her?'

'You'll never guess,' said Jack.

'Oh, good lad, you must have done well. How much? Ten pounds, fifteen?'

'I knew you wouldn't guess. What do you think of these? *Magic beans!* Plant them overnight and –'

'What!' said his mother. 'You stupid, gullible boy! You give away our only cow for a few beans!' And she smacked and scolded him. 'As for your precious beans: here they go out of the window. Now off to bed with you. There'll be no supper tonight.' And with this she sat down, and had a good cry. Jack went upstairs to bed, a sad and hungry boy.

The next morning, when Jack woke, his room looked strange. Where the sunlight usually shone in, all was dark and shady. Jack jumped out of bed and looked through the window. And would you believe it? Those beans his mother had thrown away had sprung up into an enormous beanstalk, which rose right up, and disappeared into the sky. So they were magic beans after all!

With a run and a jump, Jack was on the beanstalk and climbing up it. He climbed and he climbed and he climbed and he climbed and he climbed, till at last he reached the sky.

At the top of the beanstalk he stepped off. Before him stretched a wide road. So he walked along and he walked along till he came to a huge house. And there on the doorstep of the huge house stood a huge woman.

'Good morning, ma'am,' said Jack, as polite as could be. 'Would you be so kind as to give me some breakfast?'

'It's breakfast you want, is it?' said the huge woman. 'It's breakfast you'll *be* if you stay here much longer. My husband is an ogre, and little boys on toast are what he likes best of all. He'll be home soon; you'd better be off.' But Jack was that hungry, having missed his supper and his breakfast, he couldn't go another step. Besides, adventure was what he longed for; he wanted to stay and see this ogre.

So Jack pleaded and begged till at last the ogre's wife felt sorry for him. She took him inside and gave him bread and cheese. But Jack had barely time to eat it before he heard the ogre coming. Thump! Thump! Thump! The whole house trembled with the noise.

'Goodness, it's my husband!' said the ogre's wife. 'Quick! Jump in here!' She bundled Jack into the oven, just as the ogre came in.

Now this ogre was a big one, to be sure! He sniffed and he snuffed, and then he roared,

'Fee-fi-fo-fum,
I smell the blood of an Englishman,
Be he alive, or be he dead,
I'll grind his bones to make my
bread!'

'There's no one here,' said his wife. 'Maybe you can still smell that boy you had for supper last night. Now sit down and have your breakfast. It's all ready for you.'

So the ogre had his breakfast. After that he went to a big chest and took out some bags of gold. Down he sat and started to count till at last he fell asleep, with his head on the table. Soon his snores shook the whole house.

By and by Jack crept out of the oven, and as he passed the table he saw the bags of gold. Quickly he tucked one under his arm, and away he ran. He kept on running till he came to the beanstalk. Down he climbed and down he climbed, and finally he reached the bottom. Then he rushed in to show his mother the gold.

Well, first she hugged and kissed him, and then she scolded and smacked him. But when she saw the gold she hugged and kissed him again.

For quite a time Jack and his mother lived on the bag of gold till at last it had gone, which is the way with money. Then Jack had a mind to go up the beanstalk once more. His mother, though, didn't care for that idea. So one fine morning, before she was about, Jack started up the beanstalk. He climbed and he climbed and he climbed and he climbed and he climbed till he came to the road again. He reached the huge house and there was the huge woman on the doorstep as before.

'Good morning, ma'am,' said Jack, as bold as brass. 'Could you give me some breakfast please?'

'Aren't you the lad who came once before?' said she. 'Do you know my husband lost some gold that morning?'

'You don't say,' said Jack. 'I might be able to help you there. But I'm that hungry I can't think until I've had a bite to eat.'

When he had finished, the ogre said, 'Wife, bring me the hen that lays the golden eggs.'

At this Jack's ears pricked up and he peeped out. Then the ogre stroked the hen and said, 'Lay,' and it laid a golden egg! And again he said, 'Lay,' and it laid another!

In a while the ogre began to nod his head. When his snores shook the house Jack knew it was safe to come out. He caught hold of the hen, and was off in a flash. But as he ran out, the hen gave a cackle which woke the ogre. Jack heard him roar, but he heard nothing else. He was away, and down the beanstalk as fast as he could scramble.

When Jack got home he showed his mother the wonderful hen, and said, 'Lay,' and it laid a golden egg, as easy as that. His mother was delighted, and the two of them became very rich indeed. This time, of course, the money did not run out. But Jack couldn't settle. He had a taste for adventure now, and he was determined to go again. Still his mother wouldn't hear of it. So one fine morning Jack rose early, and up the beanstalk he climbed.

At this the ogre's wife became so curious she took Jack in and gave him something to eat. But he had scarcely started eating when – Thump! Thump! Thump! They heard the ogre coming. Into the oven went Jack again, not a minute too soon.

Everything happened just as before. In came the ogre sniffing and snuffing around the room. *'Fee-fi-fo-fum'* and all the rest. Finally his wife calmed him, and he settled down to his breakfast.

*'Fee-fi-fo-fum,
I smell the blood of an Englishman.
I smell him, wife. I smell him!'*

'Well, dear, if it's that little rogue who stole your gold and the hen that lays the golden eggs, then he's sure to be in the oven,' said his wife.

But Jack wasn't in the oven, and though they searched, they never found him.

At last the ogre sat down, and ate his breakfast, but still he grumbled and growled. Finally he called out, 'Wife, bring me my golden harp.'

Now this harp was magical, and when the ogre said, 'Sing,' the harp sang so sweetly it soothed away all his ill-temper. Soon the ogre fell asleep, and once more his snores shook the house.

Quickly Jack climbed out of the copper, and crept up to the table. He took hold of the golden harp, but it was more magical than Jack had realised. As he crept away with it, the harp cried out, 'Master! Master!'

Up and up and up and up and up till he reached the top. This time he didn't go straight to the ogre's wife, he was too smart for that. He waited behind a bush. When she came out, he crept inside and hid himself in the copper, where she washed the clothes.

He hadn't been there long when – Thump! Thump! Thump! The ogre and his wife came in. The ogre sniffed and he snuffed, and he snuffed and he sniffed.

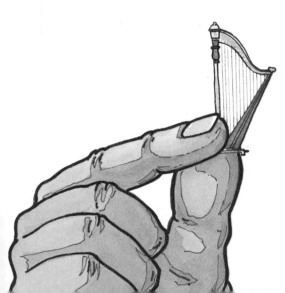

Then the ogre woke up just in time to see Jack running off with his harp. The ogre, still half asleep, stumbled out of the door. Jack raced off down the road. Behind him

Down and down and down he scrambled, in fear of his life. Then the ogre stopped for a second. He didn't like to trust his great weight to a beanstalk. Again the harp called,

came the ogre, as fast as his huge, great legs would carry him. Jack had a head start but his little legs had to work twice as hard to cover the distance. Just when he thought he couldn't run a step further, he saw the top of the beanstalk. Pausing for breath, he turned, and saw the ogre almost on top of him. The ogre reached out to snatch Jack up in his massive hand. But Jack was away down the beanstalk, in the nick of time.

'Master! Master!' With one step the ogre was on the beanstalk and coming down fast. Jack felt the beanstalk swaying wildly, and when he looked up he saw two monstrous boots above his head. Then Jack had to do something, quickly.

'Mother! Mother!' he called. 'Bring me an axe.'

Jack's mother came running with the axe, but when she saw the ogre with his legs just through the clouds, she was so flummoxed, she dropped the axe on the ground. Before she could turn round, Jack took it up, and chopped once, twice, then clean through the beanstalk. First it swayed this way, then it swayed that way, and then CRRRRASH! Down came the ogre, and hit the ground so hard that it killed him stone dead.

Well, with as much gold as they needed, and the harp to keep them always happy, there was nothing else they could wish for. Except a wife for Jack, of course. And for such a brave lad only a princess would do. So a princess he found. Then Jack, and his wife, and his mother lived happily together for the rest of their very long lives.

Sly Fox and the Little Red Hen

Once upon a time there was a smart little house, with a shiny blue door, and in the smart little house there lived a little Red Hen. She was a good, careful hen, and whenever she went out visiting she locked her shiny blue door with a little key. Then she put the key in the pocket of her apron, where she kept her scissors, and her thimble, and her needle and thread.

Now across the valley in a dark, deep wood was another little house. It was an ugly, crooked house, with a tumbledown door, and all the paint was peeling off. In that house lived sly Mr Fox. This rascal of a fox thought that the little Red Hen would make a fine supper for him. He had been trying to catch her for a long time; so long that he had grown quite thin. But at last he worked out a clever plan.

Look out little Red Hen!

The next morning Sly Fox got up very early. He put his big cooking-pot full of water over the fire. Then he slung his sack over his shoulder and off he went to little Red Hen's house. When he got there he hid behind a tree and waited. At last little Red Hen came out to collect some water. She was only going to the well, so she didn't bother to lock the door. While she was out that Sly Fox slipped into her house and hid himself.

When little Red Hen came in she shut the door – Squawk! Squawk! Squawk! What a nasty surprise! There was that rascal of a fox waiting to grab her.

Look out little Red Hen!

Quick as a wink, little Red Hen flew up onto a high beam. There she sat puffing and panting, but safe out of reach. She looked down at that sly fox. 'You may as well go home,' she said. 'You won't get me now.'

But that crafty fox wasn't beaten yet. 'We'll see about that,' he said.

Now Sly Fox knew he couldn't go up there to get little Red Hen. No, he knew he would have to find a way to get her to come down. So what do you think he did? He began to chase his tail, as fast as he could. Little Red Hen looked down and watched him.

Round and round and round he ran.
Round and round and round he ran.
Round and round and round went little Red Hen as she watched him.
Soon she got so dizzy she fell off the beam.

Down and down and down she fell.
Down and down and down she fell.
Into the sack she went – PLOP!

How that Sly Fox grinned. Then he slung his sack over his shoulder and set off home.

But it was a hot day and soon Sly Fox began to tire. He stopped by the roadside, carefully put the sack down on the grass, and fell asleep. Now little Red Hen began to wonder how she might escape. So she took her scissors, which she kept in her apron pocket, cut a hole in the sack, and climbed out. While the fox slept on, little Red Hen put three big stones into the sack, and with her thimble, and her needle and thread, she sewed up the hole with neat little stitches. Then off she ran, licketty-split, back to her own little house. She closed the door and locked it tight.

Goodness – she was so glad to be home!

Not long after that, sly Mr Fox woke up and, grabbing the sack, he went on his way. The further he walked the heavier the sack felt. He grumbled and he groaned, but then he thought, 'Never mind, this little Red Hen is heavy enough to make two meals for me!'

When he reached his house, Sly Fox was so hungry he went straight in and took the lid off his cooking-pot, which was already bubbling away over the fire.

'Now,' he thought, 'it won't be long!'

He lifted up the sack.

'What a fine meal it will be!'

He held the sack over the pot.

'Yum-yum-yum!'

And emptied out the fat, juicy . . . stones!

PLOP! PLOP! PLOP!

In went the stones — out splashed the boiling water — all over that sly Mr Fox. You should have heard him howl!

He never went after hens again, you can be sure of that.

As for little Red Hen, she lived happily in her own little house, with its shiny blue door, which she locked with her own little key — *every time* she went out.

The Three Little Pigs

Once upon a time when pigs spoke
rhyme
And monkeys chewed tobacco,
And hens took snuff to make them
tough,
And ducks went quack, quack,
quack, O!

There was an old sow who had three little pigs. One day she had no food left to give them, so she decided to send them out, into the world, to seek their fortune. She gave them lots of good advice, and as she waved them goodbye, she said, 'Be sure to look out for the big, bad wolf.'

'Oh, we will,' said the three little pigs, and away they went, each by a different road.

Quite soon the first little pig met a man carrying some straw. The little pig said, 'Please, man, give me some straw to build me a house.' So the man gave him some straw, and the little pig built his house with it. And a very nice house it looked too.

Presently, along the road came a big, bad wolf, who knocked at the door, and said, 'Little pig, little pig, let me come in!'

But the little pig said, 'No, no, by the hair of my chinny chin chin, I will not let you in!'

'Then I'll huff, and I'll puff, and I'll blow your house down!' And the wolf huffed, and he puffed, and he blew that house down, and gobbled up the first little pig.

Meanwhile, the second little pig walked along the road, until he met a man with a bundle of sticks. The second little pig said, 'Please, man, give me some sticks to build me a house.' So the man gave him some sticks, and the second little pig built his house. And very pleased he was with it too.

But soon, along the road, came the big, bad wolf, and said, 'Little pig, little pig, let me come in!'

'No, no, by the hair of my chinny chin chin, I will not let you in!'

'Then I'll huff, and I'll puff, and I'll blow your house down!' So the wolf huffed, and he puffed, and he HUFFED, and he PUFFED, and at last he blew down the house of sticks, and gobbled up the second little pig.

Meanwhile, the third little pig walked along, and he walked along, until he met a man with a load of bricks.

And the little pig said, 'Please, man, give me some bricks to build me a house.' So the man gave him some bricks, and the third little pig built his house with them. It took a long time to build, but it was a good, strong house, with a chimney, and a window, and a door that locked. When it was finished, the little pig went inside his house, and locked the door.

Just in time, for along the road came that wicked wolf! He knocked at the door, and said, 'Little pig, little pig, let me come in!'

21

Well, the little pig got up at five, and went and dug some turnips, and was safe home again by six, when the wolf came and said, 'Little pig, little pig, are you ready?'

Then the little pig said, 'Ready! Why I have been, and come back again, and the turnips are cooking for my dinner.'

When the wolf heard this he was very angry. But he was determined to get that

'No, no, by the hair of my chinny chin chin, I will not let you in.'

'Then I'll huff, and I'll puff, and I'll blow your house down!' Well, he huffed, and he puffed, and he PUFFED, and he HUFFED, and he HUFFED, and he PUFFED, but he could *not* blow that house down. So then the wily wolf thought he would have to get the little pig another way.

In his very best voice he said, 'Little pig, I know where there is a nice field of turnips.'

'Where?' asked the little pig.

'Oh, in Mr Smith's Home-field. If you will be ready, tomorrow morning early, I will take you there.'

'Very well,' said the little pig. 'What time will you come?'

'Oh, at six o'clock.'

little pig, so he said, 'Little pig, I know where there is a fine apple tree.'

'Where?' asked the little pig.

'Down at Merry Garden,' replied the wolf. 'If you'll be sure to wait for me this time, I will come for you at five o'clock tomorrow, and we'll get some apples.'

Next morning the little pig was up very early, and at four o'clock he was away down to Merry Garden. But those apples tasted so good that he ate, and ate, and was much longer than he meant to be. Just as he was about to climb down the tree, who should he see coming along the road, but that big, bad wolf!

When the wolf reached the tree he said,

However, the wolf was not going to give up. The next day he came again, and said, 'Little pig, there is a fair in town this afternoon, would you like to go?'

'Oh, yes,' said the little pig. 'When will you call?'

'At three,' said the wolf. 'Make sure you wait for me this time.'

'Why, little pig, are you here already? Are they nice apples?'

'Delicious,' said the little pig. 'Here, I'll throw you one.' And he threw it so far that the stupid wolf ran after it. Then the little pig jumped down, and ran home before the wolf could catch him.

But once again the little pig went off early, and enjoyed the fair, and bought himself a fine, big butter-churn. He was taking it home when – he saw the wolf coming up the hill towards him! Well, he was in a fine mess now, so he jumped into the butter-churn to hide. Suddenly it fell over, and started to roll down the hill. Faster and faster it rolled, with the little pig inside, squealing at the top of his voice. The wolf was so frightened, he ran all the way home, without going to the fair.

When the wolf next went to the pig's house, he told the little pig how frightened he had been by a terrible monster, which had almost knocked him down.

Then the little pig laughed, 'I thought that had frightened you. That was me! I had been to the fair and bought a butter-churn, and when I saw you coming I got inside and rolled all the way home.'

Well, this made the wolf so angry he was fit to burst. 'Now, little pig,' he roared, 'I am coming to get you! I will climb down your chimney, and come and gobble you up, every last little bit!'

But that clever little pig knew just what to do. He had already hung the big pot in the fire-place, and now he poked up his fire to

bring the water to the boil. Just as the wolf was coming down the chimney, the little pig took off the lid and in fell the wolf – SPLASHHHH! And that was the end of him!

After that the third little pig was happy in his own little house. He had as many turnips as he could eat, lots of fine rosy apples, and he often visited the fair. But as long as he lived, he was never again troubled by a big, bad wolf.

Cinderella

As though to punish the girl further, the stepsisters were given the finest clothes to wear, and the most luxurious rooms to sleep in, while the poor child had just one dull dress, and was forced to sleep in a cold attic room on a mattress of straw. Her only comfort was to rest each evening, in the chimney corner, among the ashes and cinders of the fire. And because of this they called her Cinderella. But despite her dusty, ragged clothes, Cinderella was very beautiful, a hundred times more beautiful than her stepsisters in all their finery.

Now it happened one day, that the King's son was giving a ball to which all the fashionable people in the kingdom were invited, and Cinderella's stepsisters were, of course, included. They were most excited and could talk of nothing but the ball, and the clothes they would wear. For Cinderella this meant more work than ever. She had to wash all her sisters' clothes, just in case they might choose this dress or that petticoat.

Once upon a time there was a young girl whose mother died and left her to be brought up by her father. She was a pretty, kind-hearted girl, and she had promised her mother, before she died, that she would always try to be good. So the girl and her father lived quite happily together, until the time when he married again. For his second wife, he chose a proud and spiteful woman. She also had two ugly daughters, and they were equally cruel and bad-tempered. With the three of them, the poor young girl knew not a minute's peace.

They bullied and teased her from morning till night, making her wait on them, and do all the worst jobs in the house. She swept their rooms, washed the dishes, scrubbed the floors and never complained, for she remembered her promise to be good. But this made her stepmother even more envious. The young girl's pretty looks and sweet nature made her stepsisters appear more ugly and disagreeable than ever.

They called for her and shouted at her all
day long:

'Cinderella! You must help me to decide
what to wear.'

'Cinderella! My hair needs brushing.'

'Cinderella! Come here this minute. I
want you to do my make-up.'

'Cinderella! Cinderella!'

The poor child was run off her feet, but
she accepted all this extra work without
complaint, and did her best to make her
stepsisters look as fine as possible.

While they chattered away, and sat
admiring themselves in their grand mirrors,
Cinderella was working hard. Then one sister
said, 'Cinderella, wouldn't you like to be
going to the ball?'

'Oh, very much,' said Cinderella. But then
she saw how they grinned, and she said, 'But
you are teasing me. How could I go to such
a grand ball?'

'How indeed!' the sisters sneered. 'Just
think how everyone would stare if they saw a
cinder-wench like you dancing.' And they
laughed and laughed and laughed.

Soon it was time to leave. Cinderella
watched her stepsisters drive away in a fine
carriage, and at last her own unhappiness
was too much to bear. She sat in her place
by the fire, and began to cry.

Now Cinderella had one good friend, her
godmother, and just then she chanced to
call. Her godmother asked why she was
crying. Cinderella tried to tell her, 'I
wish . . . Oh, how I wish . . .' But she
couldn't speak for her tears.

'You wish you could go to the ball, don't
you?' said her wise godmother.

'Yes, more than anything in the world,'
answered Cinderella.

'And so you shall,' said her godmother.
'Let us see what we can do. The first
problem is how to get you there.'

She led Cinderella into the garden and sent
her to find a pumpkin. Cinderella couldn't
see how a pumpkin would help, but she did
as she was told. Now, Cinderella's
godmother was a fairy, and when she took
the pumpkin she lightly touched it with her
wand. The pumpkin swelled and swelled,
until it grew into an elegant coach, which
shone like gold. Next she went to the mouse-
trap where she found six live mice.

She told Cinderella to lift the trap-door carefully, and, as each mouse ran out, she quickly tapped it with her wand. Instantly the mice turned into six fine grey horses to lead the wonderful coach. Now they needed a coachman. Cinderella went to the rat-trap. Inside was a small rat which she took to her godmother. One touch of her wand changed him into a smart coachman, dressed in livery, ready to drive the coach. Finally, Cinderella was sent to find six lizards. With a little more magic, they became six splendid footmen to ride with the coach and wait on Cinderella. She was going to travel to the ball in fine style!

'There now,' said her godmother, 'this is fit for a princess. Are you ready to go?'
'Oh, yes indeed,' said Cinderella, 'but what about my ragged dress?' Just one more touch of the wand, and at once her rags became a magnificent gown of shining satin, and on her feet were a pair of extraordinary slippers made of pure gold, in which she could dance like a fairy.

At last she was completely ready. Cinderella stepped into the coach feeling like a true princess. But before she left, her godmother warned, 'You must be home before midnight! The magic will not last a moment longer. When the clock strikes twelve, the coach will become a pumpkin, the horses mice, the coachman a rat, the footmen lizards, and your lovely clothes will turn into rags once more.' Cinderella promised to be home in time and, completely happy, she set off for the ball.

When she arrived at the palace she was introduced as a princess, and the King's son came to greet her. As he led Cinderella into the hall everyone stopped dancing, even the music stopped. The whole company stood back to admire this unknown princess. She looked so beautiful that everyone was amazed, and when she danced she charmed them even more. The Prince would dance with no one else, and sat beside her throughout the evening. There was a marvellous supper served but the Prince ate nothing; he could only gaze at Cinderella. During supper, Cinderella sat beside her stepsisters and talked with them about all manner of things, but they did not recognise her. They were flattered that the beautiful princess sat with them, never suspecting who she might be.

After supper the Prince again danced with Cinderella and paid her many compliments. She was so happy that she completely forgot the time.

Suddenly the clock began to strike twelve:
One! Two! Three! In panic Cinderella fled from the hall.
Four! Five! Six! She ran down the great staircase, never daring to look back. On the way she lost one of her gold slippers but there was no time to stop.
Seven! Eight! Nine! Away she ran, across the courtyard. She could hear voices now, and the sound of footsteps behind her, but she didn't look back.
Ten! Eleven! Twelve! And she was gone. By the time she left the palace grounds she was dressed once more in rags; all the magic had vanished. All except one of her little gold slippers, which she clutched in her hand.

Meanwhile, the Prince was in despair. He had quickly followed Cinderella but she had run so swiftly she had completely disappeared. All he found was her gold slipper lying on the stairs. Then the Prince questioned the palace guards but they had seen no one, except a ragged kitchen servant, and they never guessed who she might be. The Prince was determined to find the lovely princess, but his only clue was the gold slipper, which he held close to him for the rest of the ball.

'I wish I could have seen these grand people,' said Cinderella.

'You! Don't be ridiculous. You'll never see the Prince. A ragamuffin like you.' And the two sisters shrieked with laughter.

Well, the next day the young Prince issued a proclamation that he would marry the girl whose foot the slipper fitted. Furthermore, everyone in the kingdom would have a chance to try the slipper.

Some time later the stepsisters came home. They could talk of nothing else but the beautiful princess, who had disappeared at midnight.

'The Prince has clearly fallen in love with her,' said the first sister. 'He looked at no one else the whole evening.'

'I should think he will marry her, if he ever finds her again,' added the second sister.

First of all, the princesses tried, and then the duchesses, and after that, all the ladies of the court, but of course it was all in vain. There was only one person in the world whom this slipper would fit.

At last the slipper was brought for the two stepsisters to try. Each sister in turn tried to force her clumsy foot into the dainty slipper. They pushed and pulled and tugged, until they were red in the face, but without success. Then the Prince asked, 'Are there no other young ladies here?' Cinderella, who had watched secretly from the kitchen, stepped forward and asked if she might try. Her stepsisters burst out laughing, and said, 'Certainly not!'

But the Prince silenced them. 'Everyone must try the slipper,' he said, and he turned to Cinderella, 'Please sit down.'

Of course the slipper slid onto her foot easily, and she took the matching slipper from her pocket. Thereupon her godmother appeared, and once more transformed Cinderella's clothes into a fine gown. Then the Prince and everyone else recognised her as the beautiful princess. At this her stepsisters were amazed. They begged Cinderella to forgive them, and tried to excuse their wickedness towards her. In her goodness, Cinderella embraced them both, and said, 'From now on we must love each other as true sisters.'

Soon after, the Prince and Cinderella were married. The wedding was a grand affair and Cinderella's stepsisters were invited. They were introduced to two great lords of the court and in time they also were married. Thanks to Cinderella, who was as good as she was beautiful, everyone lived happily ever after.

Three Billy Goats Gruff

Once upon a time there were three Billy Goats, whose name was Gruff. One was called little Billy Goat Gruff; one was called middle Billy Goat Gruff; and the other, who was almost fully grown, was called big Billy Goat Gruff. Well one day the three Billy Goats wanted to go up to the hillside, where the grass grew sweet and green, to make themselves fat.

But on the way up there was a stream, and to get over the stream they had to cross a ricketty, racketty bridge.

Now under the ricketty, racketty bridge there lived a terrible Troll. The Troll was enormous, and as strong as ten men. He had big, staring eyes and his face was so ugly it would make your hair stand on end. What was worse, he threatened to eat anyone who tried to cross HIS bridge!

So there he sat, all day, waiting and listening.

'WHO'S THAT trip-trapping over MY bridge?' roared the Troll, in a terrible voice.

'Oh, it's only me, little Billy Goat Gruff,' said the first Billy Goat, in his tiny, little voice. 'I am going up to the hillside to make myself fat.'

'Oh, no you're not,' said the Troll, 'because I'm going to gobble you up!'

'Please don't eat me. I'm too little to eat,' said the Billy Goat. 'Wait till the middle Billy Goat Gruff comes; he's much bigger.'

'All right then. Be off with you!' said the Troll, and he settled down under the bridge, to wait.

So there he sat, waiting and listening. And as he waited, he thought about the juicy meal he would soon have.

By and by, along came the first Billy Goat Gruff. *Trip, trap! Trip, trap!* went his hooves on the ricketty, racketty bridge.

Quite soon, up came the third Billy Goat Gruff. *TRIP, TRAP! TRIP, TRAP! TRIP, TRAP! TRIP, TRAP!* went his hooves on the rickety, racketty bridge. The big Billy Goat was so heavy that the poor bridge creaked and groaned under him.

'WHO'S THAT TRAMPING over MY bridge?' roared the Troll, in a terrible voice.

'IT'S ME, BIG BILLY GOAT GRUFF!' shouted the third Billy Goat, who had a big, gruff voice of his own.

'Now, big Billy Goat Gruff, I'm coming to gobble you up!' said the Troll, jumping onto the bridge.

But the big Billy Goat was not afraid. He was big and strong, and he was ready for the Troll:
'Well, come along! I've got two horns,
That'll tear you apart like a bush of thorns.
I've got four hooves as hard as stones,
And I'll crush you to bits, body and bones!'

In a little while the second Billy Goat Gruff came along. *Trip, trap! Trip, trap! Trip, trap!* went his hooves on the rickety, racketty bridge.

'WHO'S THAT trip-trapping over MY bridge?' roared the Troll, in a terrible voice.

'It's only me, middle Billy Goat Gruff,' said the second Billy Goat, in his middle-sized voice. 'I am going up to the hillside to make myself fat.'

'Oh, no you're not,' said the Troll, 'because I'm going to gobble you up!'

'No, don't eat me. Wait till the big Billy Goat Gruff comes. He will make a much better meal.'

'All right then. Be off with you!' growled the Troll, and he climbed back under the bridge to wait.

So there he sat, waiting and listening! He was getting very hungry by this time, and when the Troll was hungry he was meaner and nastier than ever.

That was what the big Billy Goat said. And that was what he did. He stabbed the Troll with his sharp horns, and he crushed him with his hard hooves. Then he tossed that terrible Troll out into the stream. The Troll fell into the water like a great, big rock.

SPLASH! He sank right to the bottom!

After that the big Billy Goat went up to the hillside. There the three Billy Goats Gruff ate, and ate, and ate, until they got so fat they couldn't even walk home. And if the fat hasn't fallen off them, why they must still be there. And so...
      Snip, snap, snout,
      This tale's told out.

Sleeping Beauty

Now at this time there were thirteen fairies living in the kingdom. But one was very old, and some thought she might be dead. Besides, the King only had twelve gold plates for them to eat from, so the old fairy wasn't invited.

The feast took place and when it was over, the fairies, each in turn, gave the child their gifts. The first gave her beauty, the second grace, the third kindness, and so on until the child had everything that one could wish for. But just as the last fairy was about to speak, the old fairy appeared, and she was very much alive! Dressed all in black, and full of bitterness, she rushed into the hall and cried, 'Because you did not invite me, this shall be my gift: when your daughter is fifteen years old, she will prick her finger on a spindle and fall down dead.'

The King and Queen, and all who heard, were horrified. But the last fairy had not yet spoken. While she could not prevent the wicked gift, she could soften it.

There was once a King and Queen who longed for a child, but no child was born. The years passed, and they became more unhappy. One day, when the Queen had been bathing in the river, a frog came to her and said, 'Your wish will soon be granted. Within one year you will have a daughter.'

And it happened that the Queen had a baby girl. The King was delighted, and he ordered a great feast to be held, inviting everyone in the kingdom. In particular he asked the fairies, hoping that they might look kindly on the child.

'The Princess will not die,' the good fairy said. 'Instead she will fall into a deep sleep which will last for a hundred years.'

Even then the King was not consoled. He still hoped to save his daughter, and ordered that every spindle in the kingdom should be burned.

She was wandering here and there in the palace grounds, when she discovered an old tower. It seemed strange to the Princess that she had never seen this tower before. Her curiosity led her on. She climbed the winding staircase until she came to a little door. In the lock was a golden key, which she turned, and the door opened.

At last the King and Queen were content. The Princess grew to be perfectly beautiful, with every virtue the fairies had foretold.

But all too soon she reached her fifteenth year, and there came a day when the King and Queen were out riding, and the Princess was left alone.

Inside the room an old woman sat spinning flax. The Princess asked the old woman what she was doing, for of course she had never seen a spinning-wheel before. 'I am spinning, my dear,' said the old woman. The Princess came nearer.

She was attracted by the spindle and she put out her hand to take it. Hardly had she touched it than she pricked her finger.

Around the palace a hedge of thorns sprang up. It grew higher and higher, until within an hour the palace was entirely hidden from view. And thus the enchantment was complete.

Of course, rumours of the beautiful princess, who lay sleeping, spread through the kingdom and beyond. From time to time young princes came, thinking they might waken the Sleeping Beauty, but none of them could force a way through the forest of thorns.

At once a deep sleep descended on her. And the sleep spread throughout the palace like a fine mist.

The King and Queen, who had just returned, fell asleep on their thrones, with their courtiers sleeping around them. The servants in the kitchens, the guards at the gates, even the animals in the stables, all fell asleep where they were. Not a creature stirred, not a sound was heard.

Many long years went by until another Prince came to those parts. He heard the story of the Sleeping Beauty from an old man, who had heard the story from his grandfather.

'Inside that great hedge,' said the old man, 'they say there is a palace, where a beautiful princess lies in an enchanted sleep. And the King and Queen, and all their court, sleep too.'

36

At last he came to the old tower, and there lay the sleeping Princess. She looked so beautiful, as she lay sleeping, that the Prince fell in love with her. He bent down and kissed her, and in a moment she awoke. And the enchantment was broken.

Then the King and Queen awoke, and their courtiers, servants, and all the animals. Every creature stirred and stretched, and all was hustle and bustle throughout the palace. Each person continued just where he had left off, exactly one hundred years ago.

'Can no one wake them?' asked the Prince.

'Well, they're all waiting, they say, for a certain Prince who will break the spell.'

The young Prince listened eagerly. 'Why shouldn't I be that Prince?' he said.

But the old man warned, 'Beware! Many have tried to force their way through, but all have failed, and some have died in the attempt!'

Nevertheless the young Prince was not afraid and he set off in the direction of the palace.

It seemed that the time was now right, and as he approached the hedge of thorns, in an instant it changed to flowers. The flowers parted to let him through, then turned to thorns again behind him.

The Prince entered the courtyard of the palace and there were the guards still asleep at their posts. In the stables and barns the animals were still sleeping. And in the kitchen the servants slept where they stood, all as they had been for a hundred years.

Then the Prince passed through the great hall, where the King and Queen were asleep, with their courtiers around them. Everything was still and silent. The Prince could even hear his own breathing.

Soon after, the wedding of Sleeping Beauty and the Prince was celebrated with a great feast, and the two of them lived happily, none more happily, for the rest of their lives.

Snow White and the Seven Dwarfs

Once upon a time, in the middle of winter, a certain queen was sewing by an open window. The window-frame was made of ebony and it shone black against the snow. As she sewed, she pricked her finger and three drops of blood fell onto the snow.

When she saw the blood, the queen made a wish. She wished that she might have a child as white as snow, as red as blood, and as black as ebony. In time her wish came true: a child was born with skin as white as snow, cheeks as red as blood, and hair as black as ebony. She was named Snow White. But when the child was born the good queen died.

After a while the king took another wife, who was very beautiful, but proud and cruel. She could not bear to think that anyone else might be more beautiful. The new Queen had a wonderful mirror, and she would stand before it and say:

'Mirror, mirror on the wall,
Who is the fairest of us all?'

And the mirror always replied,

'Queen, thou art the fairest of us all.'

Then the Queen was content, for she knew the mirror could not lie.

However, Snow White was a pretty child, and she grew to be very beautiful. A time came when she grew even more beautiful than the Queen. That day the Queen stood before her mirror and said,
'Mirror, mirror on the wall,
Who is the fairest of us all?'
And the mirror replied,
'Queen, thou art fairer than most;
it is true,
But Snow White is fairer still than
you.'

Then the Queen was furious. From that moment she turned against Snow White, and she hated her. Envy grew inside her until it gave her no rest. Finally, she called a huntsman and said, 'I never want to see Snow White again. Take her into the deepest wood and kill her! Bring me her heart as proof you have done it.'

Well, the huntsman tried to obey the Queen, but he couldn't. He felt such pity for Snow White that he spared her life. But he left her in the wood, thinking that she might be eaten by wild beasts.

To satisfy the wicked Queen, he took back the heart of a wild boar, which she cooked and ate, thinking it was the heart of Snow White.

And so the poor child wandered for many hours, afraid and lost in the wood. But even though wild beasts did come near, none harmed her. At last she came to a little house and went inside to rest. Everything in the house was small, and cleaner and neater than words can tell. There was a little table laid with seven places. Against the wall seven little beds stood in a row. Snow White was hungry, but rather than leave anyone without food, she ate just a bit from each plate, and drank a sip of wine from each cup. Then Snow White lay down to rest, trying each bed in turn, until she fell asleep on the seventh bed.

Now this little cottage belonged to seven dwarfs, who worked all day digging for gold in the mountains. When it was dark they came home. They knew that someone had been there, for things were not as neat and tidy as when they had left. They could see that someone had eaten a bit of their food, and drunk a sip of their wine, and lain on their beds. Then they found Snow White asleep on the seventh bed. They gathered round her. She looked so beautiful, lying there, that they could not bear to waken her, so they left her to sleep in the little bed. The seventh dwarf slept an hour with each of the other dwarfs in turn, and in this way passed the night.

In the morning, Snow White told the dwarfs who she was and all that had happened to her. Then they asked her to stay with them; to cook and clean, and to keep their little house in order. Snow White was very happy and she agreed.

'But during the day,' said the dwarfs, 'you will be alone. Watch out for your stepmother. Soon she will know you are here; be sure not to let anyone inside.'

For a long time the Queen felt secure. Snow White was dead and she was sure that she was now the fairest of all. But one day she stood before the mirror and said,

'Mirror, mirror on the wall,
Who is the fairest of us all?'
Then the mirror answered,

'Over the hills, where the seven dwarfs dwell,
Snow White is yet alive and well.
Queen, thou art fairer than most;
it is true,
But Snow White is fairer still than you.'

At these words the Queen was more furious than ever. She knew the mirror could not lie, and that the huntsman had deceived her. She thought and thought of a way to kill Snow White. At last she disguised herself as a gypsy woman, carrying a basket of fine laces. She set off, over the hills, to the house of the seven dwarfs. She knocked at the door and called, 'Fine things for sale. Lovely laces for sale.'

When Snow White saw the basket of laces she was very tempted. She opened the door and invited the gypsy woman in. She soon chose a pretty lace for her bodice. Then the gypsy woman said,

'Child, what a sight you are. Come, let me lace you properly.' And she laced so quick and so tight, it took Snow White's breath away, and she fell down as if she were dead.

Not long after, the seven dwarfs returned. They found Snow White lying on the ground. When they lifted her they saw how tightly she was laced. They cut the laces in two, and she began to breathe. Slowly she recovered. When she told them what had happened they said, 'The old gypsy was surely your wicked stepmother. Be more careful. Don't let anyone in while we are away.'

Time passed and the Queen was quite content, until one day she stood before the mirror and said,

'Mirror, mirror on the wall,
Who is the fairest of us all?'
It answered the same as before,

'Over the hills, where the seven
dwarfs dwell,
Snow White is yet alive and well.
Queen, thou art fairer than most;
it is true,
But Snow White is fairer still than you.'

When she heard this the Queen flew into a fury. She had failed. Snow White was still alive! This time the wicked Queen was more determined. With the help of witchcraft, which she understood, she made a poisoned comb. She disguised herself as an old pedlar, and set off once more for the house of the seven dwarfs, and knocked at the door. This time Snow White looked out, and said,

'You must go away, I'm not allowed to let anyone in.'
'It doesn't hurt to look,' said the old pedlar woman, holding out the pretty comb. Once more Snow White was tempted; she opened the door, and let the old pedlar in.

Then the old woman said, 'Now, let me comb your hair properly. It's such beautiful hair.' And she began to comb. But the poison was so powerful, that hardly had the comb touched her head than Snow White fell down unconscious.

Fortunately it was almost evening, and soon the dwarfs came home. They realised what had happened, and quickly found the poisoned comb, and pulled it out. Again Snow White recovered, and told them all that had passed. Again the seven dwarfs tried to warn her to stay in the house, and let no one in at the door.

Meanwhile in her palace, the Queen stood before the mirror and said,
'Mirror, mirror on the wall,
Who is the fairest of us all?'
The mirror answered the same as before,
'Over the hills, where the seven
dwarfs dwell,
Snow White is yet alive and well.
Queen, thou art fairer than most;
it is true,
But Snow White is fairer still than you.'

At these words the Queen trembled with rage. 'Snow White shall die,' she cried, 'even if it costs me my life!' Then she went into a secret chamber where she prepared a poisoned apple. It was so beautiful; white-fleshed with a red cheek, that no one who saw it would be able to resist it.

'What are you afraid of? Do you think it is poisoned?' laughed the farmer's wife. 'Look, I'll cut it in two. You eat the red half, and I'll eat the other.' For the third time Snow White was tempted; she put out her hand to take it.

Again the Queen disguised herself, this time as a farmer's wife, carrying a basket of apples. She knocked at the door, and Snow White put her head out of the window and said, 'I can't let anyone in, the seven dwarfs told me not to.'

'That's all right,' said the farmer's wife, 'I'll soon sell these. But look – I'll give you one.' And she offered Snow White the beautiful apple.

'No, I daren't take anything,' said Snow White.

Now that apple was so cunningly made that only the red part was poisoned. Hardly had Snow White bitten it than she fell down dead. Then the wicked Queen looked at Snow White with deep hatred, and cried, 'White as snow, red as blood, black as ebony! This time the dwarfs will not wake you.'

As soon as she reached home, the Queen stood before the mirror and said,
        'Mirror, mirror on the wall,
        Who is the fairest of us all?'
And at last the mirror answered,
        'Queen, thou art the fairest of us all.'
Then her jealous heart could rest, as far as a jealous heart can ever rest.

When they came home, the dwarfs found Snow White lying on the ground. They searched and searched but found nothing, and they could not help her. The poor child was dead. They laid her down and wept for three days and nights.

But when it came time to bury her, they could not do it. It seemed as though she was just sleeping. And they made a coffin of glass, so that they could always see her, and wrote her name on it, and that she was a King's daughter. They set the coffin on the mountainside, where one of them always watched over her.

A long time passed and Snow White lay in the coffin, yet she remained as white as snow, as red as blood, and as black as ebony. But one day, by chance, a young Prince came into that part of the wood. When he saw the beautiful Snow White he fell in love with her, and said to the dwarfs, 'Let me take the coffin. I will treasure it always, for I cannot live without seeing Snow White.' At first the dwarfs refused; they couldn't bear to part with her. Then they began to pity the young Prince and at last they gave him the coffin.

The Prince called his servants and bade them carry it away on their shoulders. Now it happened that as they walked they stumbled and with the shaking, the bit of poisoned apple flew out of Snow White's throat. In a moment she opened her eyes and was awake.

'Where am I?' she cried.

Then the young Prince told her what had happened and said, 'I love you more than anything in the world.

Come to my father's castle and you shall be my wife.' And Snow White loved him too. She went with him, and the wedding was celebrated with a splendid feast.

Among those invited to the wedding was Snow White's evil stepmother. Dressed in her finest clothes she stood, once more, before the mirror and said,
> 'Mirror, mirror on the wall,
> Who is the fairest of us all?'
And the mirror answered,
> 'Queen, thou art fairer than most;
> it is true,
> But the young queen outshines even
> you.'

Then the Queen's fury knew no bounds, but her envy and curiosity were so great that she could not rest until she saw the young bride. As soon as she entered the hall she recognised Snow White and the fear and horror she felt fixed her to the spot. As her punishment, red-hot iron slippers had been prepared and she danced in these until she was dead.

Red Riding Hood

Once upon a time there was a little girl. She was a good little girl, as little girls go, and everyone loved her dearly. Her grandmother was particularly fond of her, and made her a beautiful red cape and hood, which the little girl wore wherever she went. So they called her Little Red Riding Hood.

One day her mother said, 'Little Red Riding Hood, your grandmother is ill. I want you to take her some cake and a bottle of wine.'

'Yes, Mother,' said Little Red Riding Hood, and she put on her cape and hood.

'Go straight there, as quickly as you can,' said her mother, 'and mind you don't wander from the path.'

'No, Mother,' promised Little Red Riding Hood, and off she went.

Now to get to her grandmother's house, Little Red Riding Hood had to walk through a thick wood. But it was a fine day, and she walked happily along, trying to catch up with her shadow.

Suddenly she came face to face with a Wolf! He was standing by the path, and he stepped out as she passed. However she did not *know* what a wicked animal he was, so she was not afraid of him.

'Good morning, Little Red Riding Hood. Where are you going?' said the Wolf, in a soft voice.

'I am going to my grandmother's house,' said Little Red Riding Hood. 'She is ill and I'm going to look after her.'

'And where does your grandmother live?' asked the Wolf.

'In the little house in the middle of the wood,' said Little Red Riding Hood. 'Surely you must know it.'

Then that wicked Wolf thought to himself, 'This sweet little girl will make a tasty meal for me, but, if I am really clever, I should be able to eat her up, and the old woman too.'

So he said, 'Why not pick some of these lovely flowers for your poor old grandmother? They would make her feel better.'

Little Red Riding Hood thought this was a good idea. And she wandered from the path, deep into the wood, where the prettiest flowers grew.

Meanwhile the cunning Wolf went straight to the grandmother's house, and knocked at the door.

'Who is it?' asked the old woman.

'It's Little Red Riding Hood,' called the Wolf, in a high voice. 'Can I come in?'

'Lift the latch, dear, and let yourself in,' she replied.

And that was just what he did. In he went, straight to the bed, and without another word, gobbled up the old woman, clothes and all. In one gulp she was gone. Then the Wolf found another nightgown and cap, got into the bed, and pulled the covers right up to his nose.

By now Little Red Riding Hood had picked as many flowers as she could carry. Soon she realised how far from the path she had wandered, and quickly set off again for her grandmother's house. When she got there, she was surprised to find the door standing open. Little Red Riding Hood went inside and saw her grandmother in bed with the covers pulled up high, looking very strange indeed.

Little Red Riding Hood came closer.
'Oh, Grandmother, what big ears you have got!' she said.
'All the better to hear you with, my dear,' was the reply. Little Red Riding Hood came closer.
'Oh, Grandmother, what big eyes you have got!'
'All the better to see you with, my dear.' Then Little Red Riding Hood came closer still, until she was standing right by the bed.
'Oh, Grandmother, what big teeth you have got!'
'All the better to eat you with, my dear!' snarled the Wolf.

Throwing back the bedclothes, he jumped out of bed, opened his huge jaws, and gobbled up Little Red Riding Hood, clothes and all, in one mouthful. And that was two of them gone. Then that wicked Wolf got back into bed, and fell fast asleep. Soon he was snoring loudly.

So there they were. The Wolf asleep in the bed, full to bursting, and inside the Wolf, Little Red Riding Hood and her poor old grandmother.

As luck would have it, a wood-cutter was passing by, and heard the thunderous snores. He thought he would look inside to see if anything was wrong. The wood-cutter went into the house. There was the Wolf, in Grandmother's bed, still wearing her clothes. 'At last!' thought the wood-cutter. 'I have long been waiting for a chance to catch this old Wolf.'

With one blow of his axe, the wood-cutter killed the Wolf. And that was the end of him! But then the wood-cutter thought, 'Perhaps the Wolf has swallowed the old woman whole. I might yet save her.'

Carefully he cut open the Wolf, and imagine his surprise when Little Red Riding Hood jumped out, and cried, 'Oh, how dark and frightening it was inside the Wolf!'

Next her grandmother came out alive, but very weak. Little Red Riding Hood helped her into bed, and gave her some cake and wine, and soon she felt much better.

And as for Little Red Riding Hood, she'd had such a terrible fright that she never again wandered from the path when she walked through the woods alone.

Rumpelstiltskin

There was once a miller, who had no money, and no brains either, but he did have a beautiful daughter. She was the apple of his eye, and no mistake. He would boast about her to anyone who would listen, until one day he went too far.

The miller had some business with the King, and when it was settled, wanting to impress the King, he said, 'Your Highness, I have a daughter.'

The King, who was not interested in the daughter of a poor miller, began to look bored.

'My daughter,' said the miller, 'is as beautiful as the day is long.'

'Mmmm,' said the King, looking very bored.

'And clever – she's as sharp as a needle!' added the miller.

By now the King was hardly listening at all, but the miller grew more excited and said, 'And talented – why she can – she can even spin straw into gold!'

Spin straw into gold! That had really done it. Now the King was listening right enough. He looked straight at the miller and said, 'Listen here, miller, you must send your daughter to me. If she can do as you say she shall be my wife. On the other hand, if you've lied to me she shall die!'

So now the miller was in a fine mess, but there was no getting out of it. His daughter had to go, though she wasn't happy about it, I can tell you. When the girl reached the palace the King led her straight to a big room. There was nothing in the room but a stool, a spinning-wheel, and lots and lots of straw. Then the King said, 'Now let's see if you're really as clever as your father says. You've got till tomorrow morning to spin this straw into gold. If you don't – well, it'll be off with your head!' And away he went, locking the door, and taking the key with him.

Poor girl! What should she do? She looked at the straw and she looked at the spinning-wheel. Oh dear! She knew she couldn't do it, so there was no point starting. But she couldn't bear to think about dying. She threw her apron over her head and sobbed. All of a sudden she heard a scritch-scratching noise at the window. Up she got and opened it, and in leapt a strange wee scrap of a man, with a wicked face and a long rusty beard. He looked up at her, right curious, and said, 'What are you crying for, miller-maid?'

'Who are you?' says she.
'Never you mind,' says he.
'Then why should I tell you?' says she.
'You've nothing to lose,' says he. And that was true enough, so she told him the tale first and last, and added, 'And it can't be done' – then she set about crying again.
'Can't be done! Who says it can't be done? I can do it,' says he. 'But what will you give me if I do?'

She had little to offer, just a necklace, but it seemed to please him. As she held it out he snatched it with his greedy little fingers and said, 'Now, out of my way. I've work to do.'

Well, he sits himself down at the wheel, flings his beard over his shoulder, and he's off. Whirl! Whirl! Whirl! Three times round and the bobbin's full of shining gold. As easy as that. Then – Whirl! Whirl! Whirl! and that's another one. In less than no time all the bobbins are full, and there's not a wisp of straw to be seen. As soon as he's done, off he goes into the night.

Come the morning, in walks the King. Now he was a bit of a miser, and gold was what he liked best in the world. When he saw the bobbins full of gold, of course, he wanted more. So he led the miller's daughter to a bigger room. There was nothing in that room but a stool, a spinning-wheel, and heaps and heaps of straw. Again he ordered her to spin it all by morning, if she wanted to keep her head! And didn't she though! This time she was in despair. She'd been lucky once, but twice was too much to hope for. Then all of a sudden there was a scritch-scratching at the window. Up she got and opened it, and in leapt that wee scrap of a man, just as before.

'Well, I see you need my help again,' says he, grinning and puffing out his nasty little chest. 'What will you give me this time?'

'I've only got this ring left,' says she, hopefully. That seemed to suit, for he snatches it off her, and settles down to work without another word. Whirl! Whirl! Whirl! So fast it makes her dizzy to watch him. By the morning there are the bobbins full of shining gold. And the straw? There isn't a wisp of it left.

When the King saw the gold he was pretty pleased with her, as you might expect.

But would you ever believe it; he still wanted more. He led the miller's daughter to yet another and even bigger room. There was nothing in this room but a stool, a spinning-wheel and an absolute mountain of straw.

Then he said, 'Right, my dear, spin all this straw into gold, and you shall be my wife. But if you fail — it'll be the end of you!'

Well, the girl was vexed now. She couldn't see how she could get out of this one, unless that horrid little man came again. Sure enough, there was the scritch-scratching at the window. When she let him in this time he was fair puffed up with conceit, and grinning from ear to ear. 'So you want to be Queen, do you?' he sneered. 'Well, I can help you,' and he grinned, 'if you want me to!'

'But I've nothing left to give you,' said she.

'Then you'll have to promise me something —'

'Anything, anything,' she cried, too hasty by half.

'Promise me that when you are Queen, you will give me your first baby.'

'Oh yes, anything, just get on with it, please.' Now, that was a bit rash. I mean she hadn't really thought about it. Still, she might never get to be Queen, and, if she did, she might not have a child. Anyway, what else could she do? If he didn't help her she'd die for sure, so that settled it.

Come the morning, in walks the King, and at last he's happy. He has a beautiful girl to marry, and more gold than he'd ever dreamed of. So they were straightaway wed.

They were pretty happy, the pair of them, and by the time a year had passed the King and Queen had a fine baby boy, and they didn't half dote on him. Then, one day when the Queen was alone with the child, who should appear before her but that strange wee scrap of a man. He grinned at her, and showed all his nasty teeth. Then he stretched out his greedy little hands and said, 'That baby's mine. I've come to take him!'

Well, the Queen was terrified, and clutched the baby to her. She'd forgot all about that horrid wee man, and the terrible promise she'd made. She begged and pleaded, and offered him all the riches of the kingdom if he would let her keep her baby.

'No, that won't do,' said he. 'What do I want with riches? A human child is worth more to me. Come on, a promise is a promise!'

Now didn't the Queen take on; weeping and wailing something dreadful. At last the cunning little man saw how he might do even better out of this, and he said, in a wheedling voice, 'Ah well, it seems a shame to part a baby from its mammy. I'll tell you what I'll do; I'll give you another chance. Three days you can have to find my name, and three guesses each day. If you guess it you can keep the child but — if you fail, then I'll take the baby *and* you my bonny Queen. Guess me in nine or you'll both be mine!' And away he went exceedingly pleased with himself.

That night the poor Queen hadn't a wink of sleep. She tossed and turned, and thought of all the unusual names she'd ever heard. It couldn't be any ordinary name, that was for certain. When the next day came she sent messengers throughout the kingdom to collect any more names they could find. But the girl still had to choose just three before the little man came.

At dusk he appeared, grinning as always. 'Now, what's my name?' says he.

'Is it Samuel?' says she.

'No, it ain't,' says he.

'Is it Ezekiel?' says she.

'No, it ain't,' says he.

'Then it must be Habakkuk,' says she.

'Oh no, it ain't,' says he, and grins that terrible grin.

The second day the Queen asked everyone around for all the fairy names they knew, and when he came that evening she thought she might have it.

'Now my beauty, what's my name?' says he.

'Is it Skillywidden?' says she.

'No, it ain't,' says he, and he grins.

'Could it be Tankerabogus?' says she.

'No, it ain't,' says he, and he grins wider.

'Well, is it – Grimeygobbler?' says she.

'No, it ain't that neither,' says he, and he grins fit to crack his face. Then he looks at her with eyes like coals of fire, and he says, 'Well, my beauty, there's only tomorrow night, then you'll both be mine. Hee, hee, hee. Mine, mine, mine!' And away he went laughing and shrieking.

Poor girl, she was just about at the end of her tether. She couldn't think what else to do. Out went the messengers again, but she had little hope really. Just before dusk, when the little man was due to come, the last of the Queen's messengers came home. He hadn't any new names for her, but he had seen something right strange on his travels. And this is what he told her; 'I was riding alone, through a wood I'd never seen before.

'There was an old cottage, a real tumbledown place, in a little clearing. And before it was a fire blazing away, and dancing round the fire was a strange wee scrap of a man. He was in a fine wild mood, prancing and dancing, and singing a song. Now how did it go?
Tonight I brew, tonight I bake,
Tomorrow the Queen and her baby I take.
I shall surely win this game,
For RUMPELSTILTSKIN is my name!'

Well that was good news and no mistake. The Queen could hardly wait for the little man to come. But when he did she pretended to be real worried. He leapt into the room, grinning from ear to ear, and oooh, his little black eyes were shining! 'Now then, my dear,' says he, 'what's my name?'

'Oh, oh, is it Abe?' says she.

'No, it ain't,' says he, and he steps towards her.

'Oh well, is it — could it be Zeb?' says she.

'No, it ain't,' says he, grinning fit to burst. Then he comes even closer, and says, 'Take your time, my beauty. One more guess, and you're both mine.'

And he stretches out his little grabbing hands. Then she steps back a pace or two, and bursts out grinning herself, and points her finger at him and says, 'Then how about — RUMPELSTILTSKIN!'

'Who told you that? Who told you that?' the little man shrieked. He stamped and carried on. Then BANG! straight through the floor he stamped his right foot. And BANG! straight through the floor went his left foot. Then WHOOSH! into the hole he went, down, down, down, down, down. And —

As sure as five and five make ten, Nobody ever saw him again.

57